The Daily News

VII - No. 5713   Tuesday, November 1,

VIET CRISIS GROWS

North Vietcong vs South Viet Minh

The Journal

1969

Monday, November

V03, XVI - No. 2507

NO PEACE NO HON

Soldiers Accused of Village M

The Post

Monday, March 8, 1965

VIETNAM WAR

Americans Land in Vietnam

The Chronicle

VOI, XII - No. 4585   Wednesday, April 30, 197

THE WAR IS OV

Saigon Renamed Ho Chi Minh City

The
Paper Boat

THAO LAM

Owlkids Books

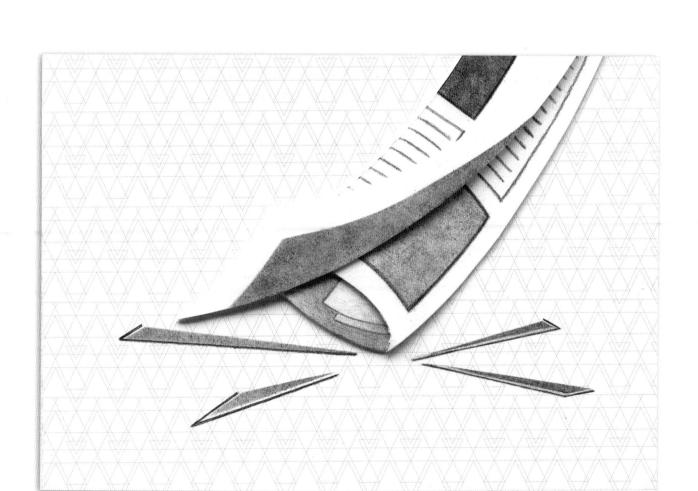

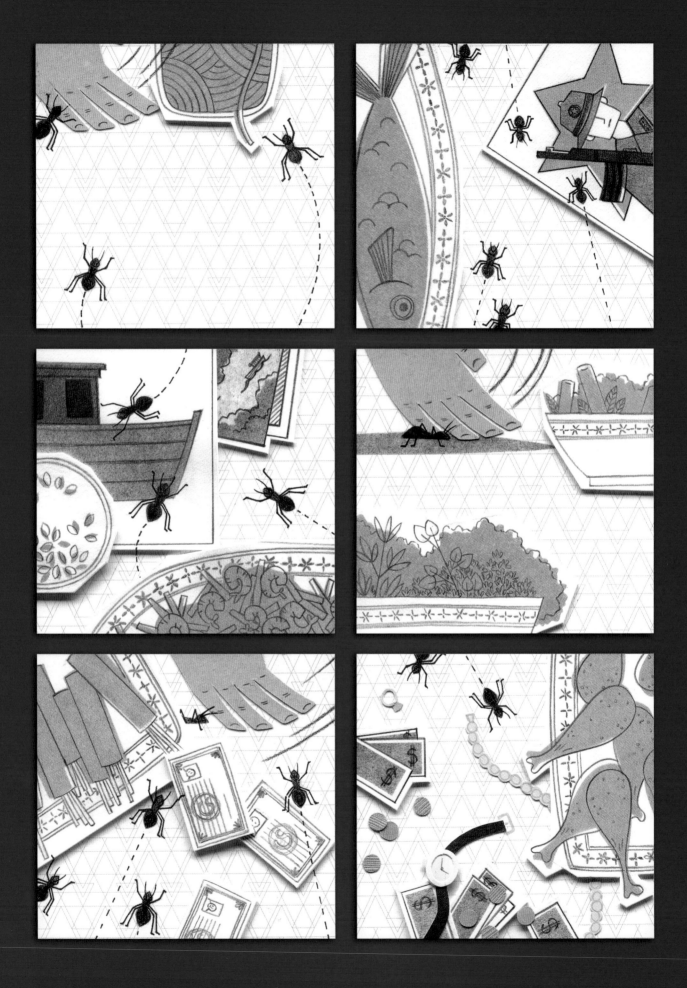

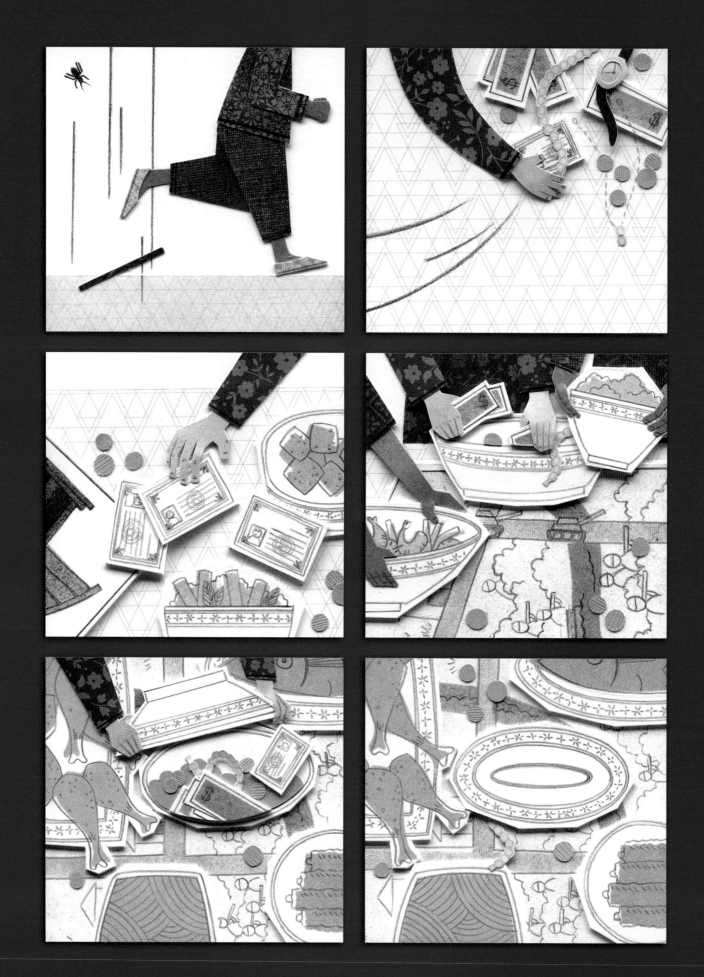

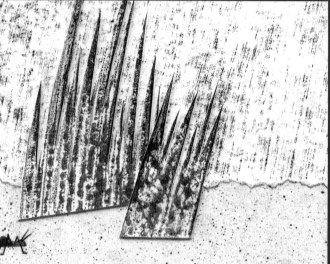

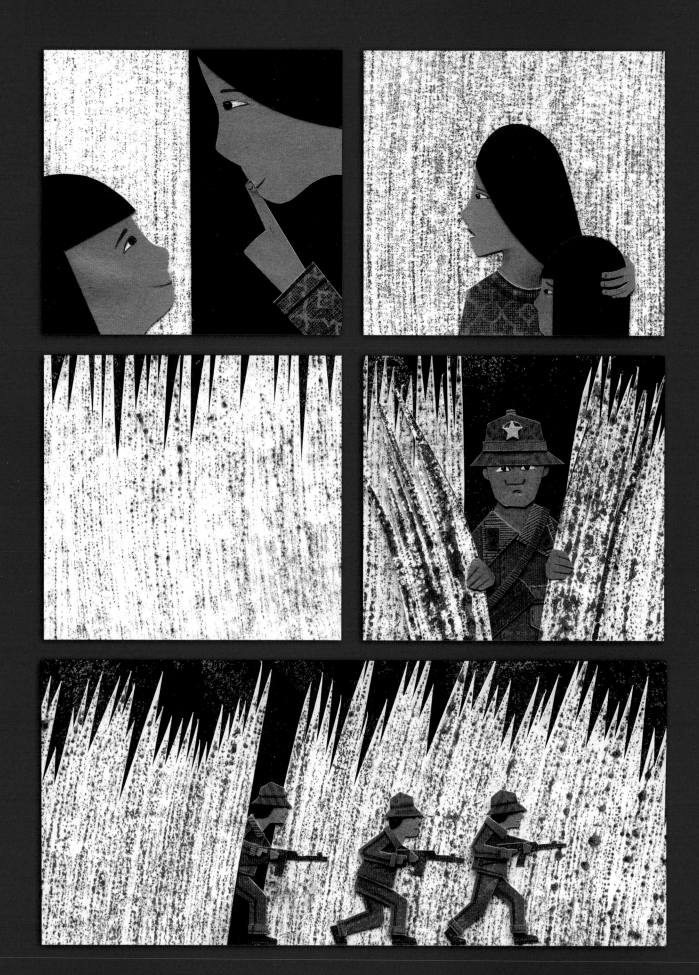

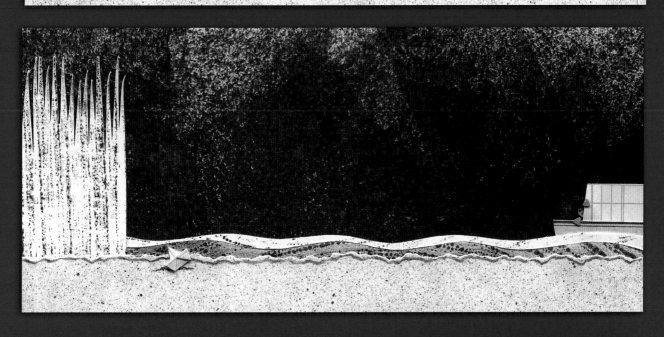

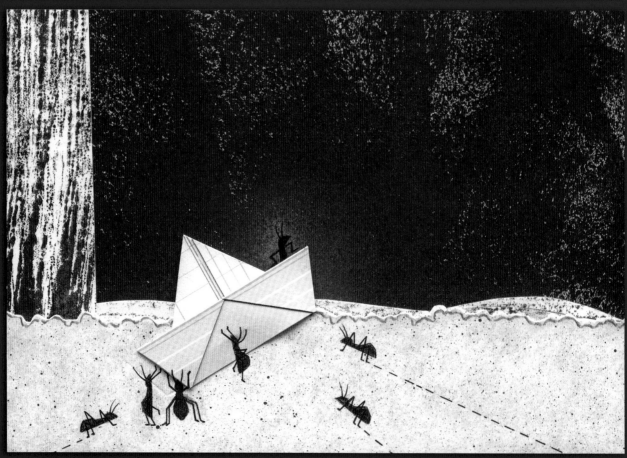

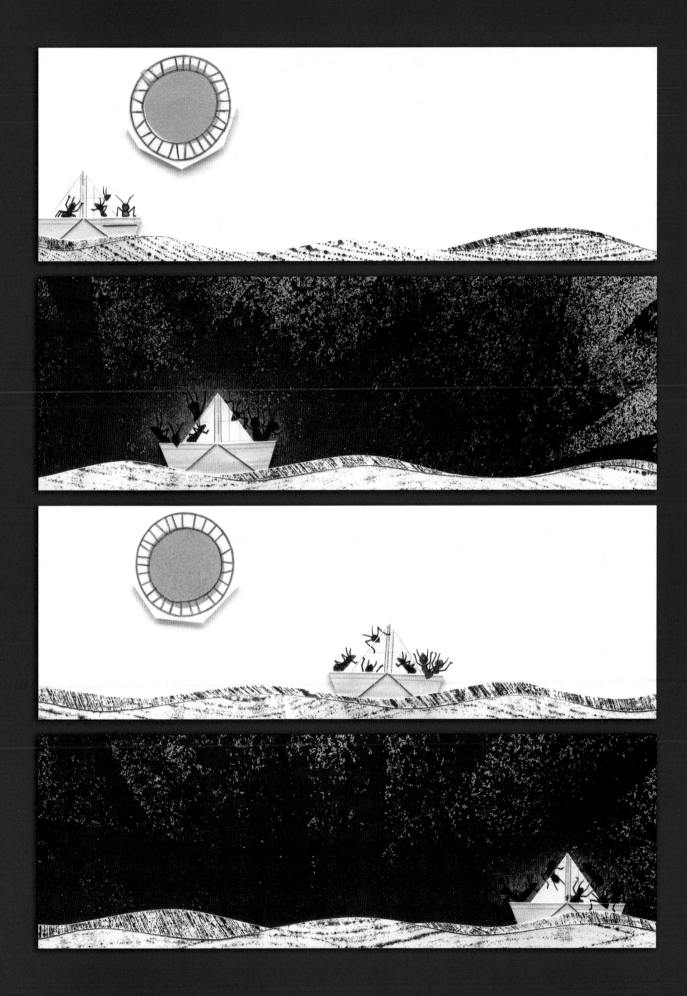

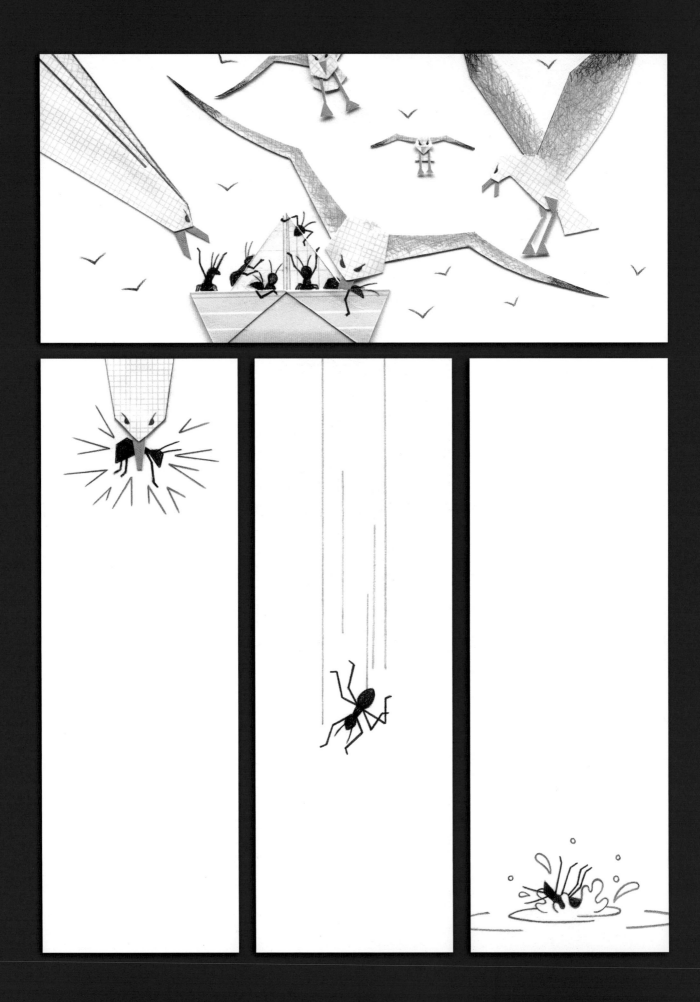

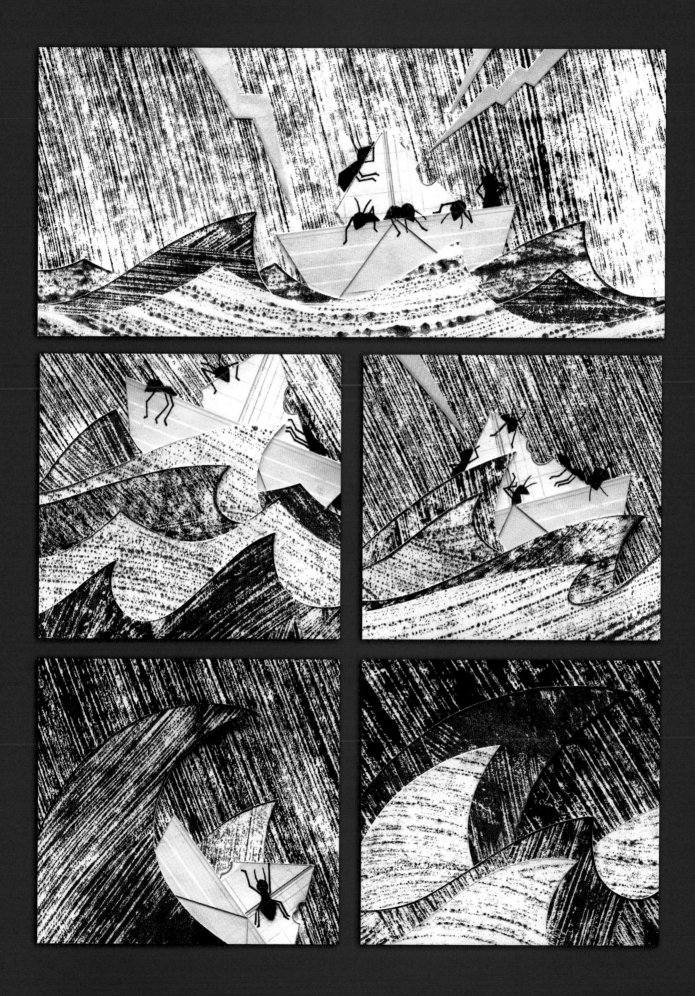

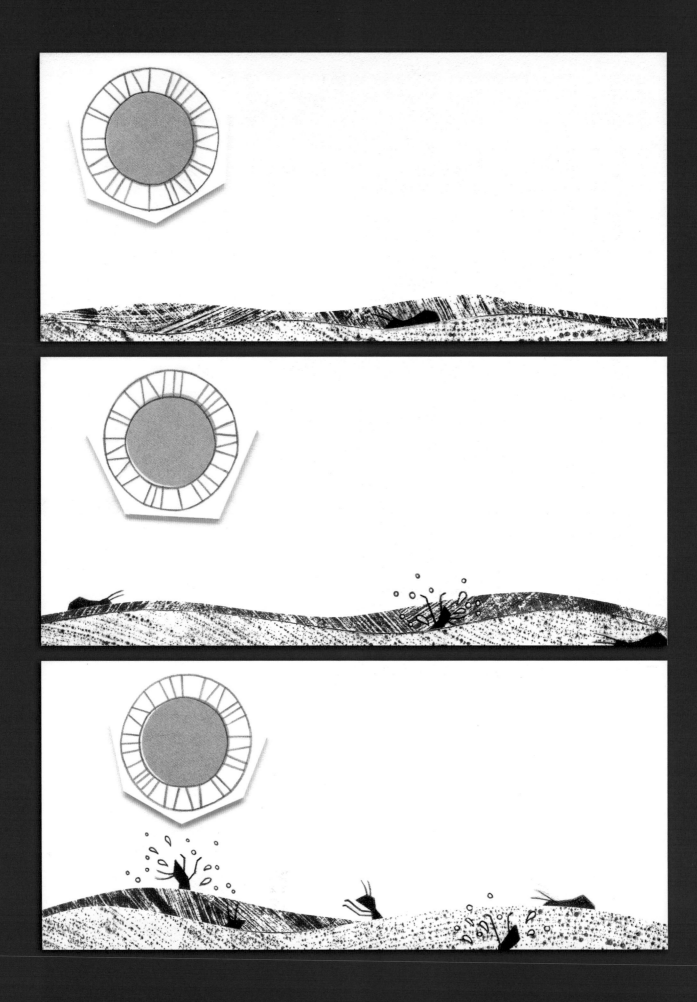

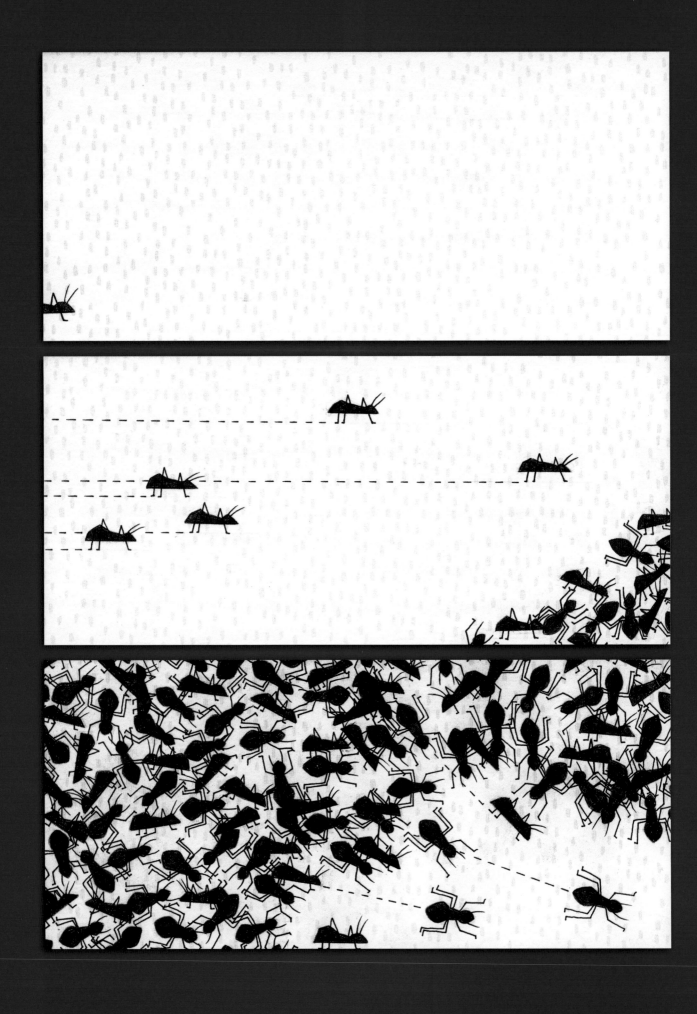

Author's Note

I was two when my family fled Vietnam. Cornered by fear and desperation, my parents risked the unknown. They boarded a small fishing boat with twenty-seven other passengers. Actually, twenty-eight—my mother, afraid of being left behind, did not tell my father she was three months pregnant with my sister. I have no recollection of this time. For years, I didn't understand the sad silence that followed my questions about the war and our journey across the South China Sea.

At the end of the Vietnam War, supporters of the South Vietnamese government were persecuted by the triumphant North Vietnamese guerrilla fighters, called the Vietcong. Death tolls continued to rise even after the war ended. Over 1.6 million refugees escaped Vietnam, the majority by boat, with nothing more than their emotional baggage and horrific memories. Both my parents left family behind.

It is estimated that 400,000 Vietnamese people died at sea from starvation, dehydration, pirate attacks, illness, and exposure to the elements. Those who survived the voyage found themselves in overcrowded refugee camps with food shortages, poor sanitary conditions, and no running water.

After four days at sea, my parents and I landed in Malaysia. For five months, we lived in a refugee camp with thousands of others seeking asylum. The lines were long as people waited to have their papers processed; with each passing day, their despair and uncertainty grew. My parents were eventually given the choice of resettling in Australia, Canada, or the United States. They decided to rebuild their life in Canada.

For the longest time, all I knew about the war and our escape was a magical story woven by my mother. Long before the war, she said, the only invasions were by ants looking for food. Her mother would set out bowls of sugar water to rid the house of the pests. As a child, Mom spent carefree afternoons rescuing them. In return, the ants rescued her when we fled Vietnam. That night, she'd got lost in the tall grass. By the light of the moon, she spotted a trail of ants and followed them … to a riverbed where our escape boat waited.

As I pieced together my family's journey to Canada, I was struck by the traits shared by ants and refugees. As one of nature's smallest creatures, ants must often move and rebuild their colonies when they're attacked or their homes are destroyed. Like refugees, ants have scattered to all parts of the world (except the North and South Poles, which are too cold). Wherever they find themselves, they adapt, contribute, and make a substantial impact on the local environment. Working together, they show great determination and resilience in tough times. They have no fear of hardship and are willing to sacrifice themselves to ensure the safety of their families above all else.

Every family has stories that are told and retold. My mother told me this one as a lesson in kindness and karma. And now I am retelling it to my little one, as a story about how deep her roots run, and about the strength and courage of the people she calls Grandpa and Nana.

When looking for strength and courage, I often picture my mother pregnant with my sister and stranded at sea with me.

_____

My first and only baby photo, taken in a Malaysian refugee camp.

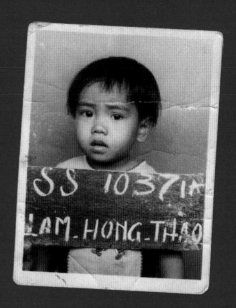

Text and illustrations © 2020 Thao Lam

Owlkids Books acknowledges the financial support of the Canada Council for the Arts, the Ontario Arts Council, the Government of Canada through the Canada Book Fund (CBF), and the Government of Ontario through the Ontario Creates Book Initiative for our publishing activities.

Published in Canada by Owlkids Books Inc., 1 Eglinton Avenue East, Toronto, ON M4P 3A1
Published in the US by Owlkids Books Inc., 1700 Fourth Street, Berkeley, CA 94710

Library of Congress Control Number: 2019956952

Library and Archives Canada Cataloguing in Publication

Title: The paper boat / Thao Lam.
Names: Lam, Thao, author, illustrator.
Identifiers: Canadiana 20200155628 | ISBN 9781771473637 (hardcover)
Classification: LCC PS8623.A466 P37 2020 | DDC jC813/.6—dc23

Edited by Karen Li
Designed by Alisa Baldwin

Manufactured in Shenzhen, Guangdong, China, in April 2020, by WKT Co. Ltd.
Job #19CB2644

A   B   C   D   E   F

 ONTARIO ARTS COUNCIL
CONSEIL DES ARTS DE L'ONTARIO
an Ontario government agency
un organisme du gouvernement de l'Ontario

 Canada Council for the Arts   Conseil des Arts du Canada

Canadä

 Publisher of Chirp, Chickadee and OWL
www.owlkidsbooks.com

| Owlkids Books is a division of  bayard canada